W9-CNA-352

AVAILABLE NOW
from Lerner Publishing Services!

The *On the Hardwood* series:

Atlanta Hawks	*Los Angeles Lakers*
Boston Celtics	*Memphis Grizzlies*
Brooklyn Nets	*Miami Heat*
Chicago Bulls	*Minnesota Timberwolves*
Cleveland Cavaliers	*New York Knicks*
Dallas Mavericks	*Oklahoma City Thunder*
Denver Nuggets	*Phoenix Suns*
Detroit Pistons	*Philadelphia 76ers*
Golden State Warriors	*Portland Trail Blazers*
Houston Rockets	*San Antonio Spurs*
Indiana Pacers	*Utah Jazz*
Los Angeles Clippers	*Washington Wizards*

Hoop City   *Long Shot*

Basketball fans: *don't miss these hoops books from MVP's wing-man, Scobre Educational.*

These titles, and many others, are available at www.scobre.com.

ON THE HARDWOOD

DENVER NUGGETS

ZACH WYNER

On the Hardwood: Denver Nuggets

MVP Books
2255 Calle Clara
La Jolla, CA 92037

MVP Books is an imprint of Scobre Educational, a division of Book Buddy Digital Media, Inc.,
42982 Osgood Road, Fremont, CA 94539

MVP Books publications may be purchased for
educational, business, or sales promotional use.

Cover and layout design by Jana Ramsay
Copyedited by Susan Sylvia
Photos by Getty Images

ISBN: 978-1-61570-906-9 (Library Binding)
ISBN: 978-1-61570-905-2 (Soft Cover)

TABLE OF CONTENTS

Chapter 1
HEADS HELD MILE HIGH

For the Denver Nuggets and their fans, May 2nd, 2013 was a day that won't soon be forgotten. It was Game 6 of the Nuggets first-round series against the Golden State Warriors, and the Denver Nuggets desperately needed a win to keep their record-setting season alive.

Owners of the best home record in basketball during the regular season, the Nuggets had lost Game 2 of the series before a stunned Pepsi Center crowd in Denver. Fans were disappointed not only because their team had lost, but because they hadn't really resembled the team that had been running opponents off their home floor all season long. When the Nuggets returned to Denver for Game 5, fans were relieved to

see a familiar sight—the Nuggets squad that had gone 38-3 at home that season. They played physical basketball, drained ten three-pointers and assisted on 26 of their 38 field goals. Young stars Ty Lawson, Kenneth Faried, and Wilson Chandler

Kenneth Faried rises high for a huge dunk.

7

Ty Lawson's penetration collapses the defense and he passes to an open teammate.

followed the lead of veteran Andre Iguodala and the Nuggets beat the Warriors, extending the series to a sixth game.

The series returned to Oakland for Game 6 and Warriors fans showed the country that they were just as hungry for a playoff series victory as the fans in Denver. But despite a wild Oracle Arena crowd, the Nuggets continued their high level of play through the first half.

At halftime, they owned a 42-40 lead. If they could just hold off the Golden State charge, they would be headed back home for Game 7. Then the tides turned. The Warriors got hot, drilled their threes, and built an 18-point lead. The Golden State bench was dancing, fans were screaming, a deafening wave of yellow and blue seemed to drown the Nuggets' hopes. But this Denver team was a proud group. As long as time remained on the clock, they were not about to hang their heads and mourn the end of their season.

Nine minutes from elimination, the Nuggets sprang to life. Lawson used his dribble penetration to break down the Warriors' defense, Iguodala sank a barrage of threes, and the Nuggets went on a 13-0 run. The Warriors pushed back, but down the stretch, when Denver forced five turnovers in a 76-second span, they cut the lead to two. In the closing seconds, Denver had the ball with a chance to tie or take the lead. Wilson Chandler missed a difficult teardrop from eight feet out, got his own rebound, and missed the put back. The Warriors held on to win the most thrilling first round series in recent memory.

When the 2012-13 Denver Nuggets walked off the Oracle Arena floor in defeat, they did so with their dignity intact. Yes, they had expected more from the playoffs than a first round loss. Yes, they had worked tirelessly all season to overcome the previous season's disappointment—a gut-wrenching Game 7 loss to the Los Angeles Lakers. But nothing could take away all that they had accomplished. The Nuggets had won the most regular-season games in franchise history. They had managed to sustain a high level of play even when their second-leading scorer, Danilo Gallinari, went down for the season with an ACL injury. In the end, they came within

Lawson congratulates Warrior guard Jarrett Jack.

one shot of forcing a Game 7 after trailing a talented Warriors team 3-1.

In the coming seasons, with the return of Lawson, Gallinari, Chandler, and Faried, and the signing of new head coach Brian Shaw, Denver fans have reason to be hopeful. The Nuggets have one of their most talented core groups since their early days in the ABA.

In 1967, there was no real demand for basketball in Denver. In fact, Denver only got the team because the owners could not find a suitable home arena in the city originally selected for the team—Kansas City. The original name of the team—the Denver Larks—didn't stick either.

Danilo Gallinari uses superior size and strength to post up Chris Paul.

Team owners ran into financial difficulties and trucking mogul Bill Ringsby bought a majority share of the Larks for $350,000. Ringsby then renamed the team the Rockets after his company's long-haul trucks. The Rockets' original uniforms bore the same logo and colors as the trucking company.

The Rockets' first season in Denver was surprisingly successful. With the United States engaged in an unpopular war in Vietnam and the Civil Rights movement in full swing, the country was in turmoil. Perhaps, at that point in time, a professional sports team was exactly what the people of Denver needed: something to rally around and feel good about,

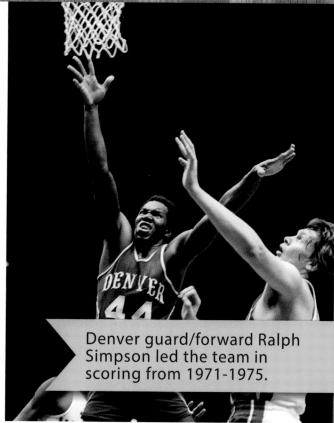

Denver guard/forward Ralph Simpson led the team in scoring from 1971-1975.

a welcome distraction from the bleakness of the evening news. The Denver Broncos, now one of the most successful and beloved professional football teams in the country, had yet

Two Sport Star

Lonnie Wright of the AFL's Denver Broncos signed with the Rockets during their first season, becoming the first player to play professional football and basketball in the same season.

to gain much of a following. With the Denver Rockets making the playoffs in each of their first three seasons, residents of the Mile High City responded. Home games averaged over 4,000 spectators and players like Ralph Simpson, Larry Jones, Willy Murrell, Byron Beck, and Wayne Hightower became household names.

In 1974, intent on moving to the NBA, the Rockets changed their name to the "Nuggets," as the name "Rockets" was already in use. Their next move was to hire a head coach who (as a player) had helped knock them out of the playoffs back in 1969. This man was Larry Brown. Now a Hall of Famer, Coach Brown is considered one of the game's great teachers. Under his tutelage, the 1974-75 team won 65 games.

The following season, David Thompson, Marvin Webster, Bobby Jones, and new teammate Dan Issel, made it all the way to the 1976 ABA Finals. In Issel, the Nuggets had found a remarkably durable and high-scoring forward/center who would become a

Larry Brown directs the offense from the sidelines.

fixture in Denver for the next 10 years. Too small to post up larger centers and not athletic enough to jump over them, Issel had developed a lethal outside shot. Combined with an awkward but effective head fake and the ability to drive to the hoop, Issel's accurate shooting made him a nearly unstoppable scorer. In fact, by the time he retired in 1985, Dan Issel was the fifth highest scorer in NBA history.

Unfortunately for Larry Brown's team, Julius "Dr. J" Erving and the New York Nets were waiting in the 1976 ABA Finals to greet them. Much like the 2012-13 Nuggets, Denver was unable to overcome a Game 2 loss at home and the Nets defeated them four games to two.

Dan Issel launches a high-arcing jump shot over the hands of a defender.

Chapter 2
THE SKYWALKER AND
THE TRADE

In 1977, the NBA and ABA merged. Four of the ABA's most successful teams (Nuggets, Pacers, Spurs, and Nets) were permitted to join the NBA. Having arrived on the big stage, the Nuggets weren't shy about carving out a space for themselves. In their first two seasons in the NBA, the Nuggets won the Midwest Division. In 1978, they made it all the way to the Western Conference Finals. Instrumental to their run was the inspired play of David "Skywalker" Thompson.

A star at North Carolina State University, Thompson led the Wolfpack to an undefeated season in 1973 and a national championship in 1974. Nicknamed "Skywalker" because of his incredible leaping ability (Thompson's vertical leap was 44 inches), he and teammate Monte Towe were the first tandem ever to execute the alley-oop pass during a game. Although dunking was not allowed in college basketball when Thompson played, he soared above the competition and wowed college hoops fans nationwide.

As a member of the Denver

Thompson graces the cover of *The Sporting News* before leading his team to the national championship.

Legendary Leaper

Legend had it that David Thompson could grab a quarter off the top of the backboard and leave behind two dimes and a nickel.

Nuggets, David Thompson turned in arguably his best season as a pro in 1978. He led the team with 27.2 points, 4.9 rebounds, and 4.5 assists per game. He was named to the NBA All-Star team as well as the All-NBA first team, and he provided one of the most dramatic runs at the scoring title in the history of the league.

On the final day of the 1978 season, Skywalker awoke second in the league in scoring. Trailing George "The Iceman" Gervin by an incredibly slim margin, Thompson figured that with a big game on his final day, the scoring title would be his. The Nuggets had already guaranteed themselves a spot in the playoffs. For Thompson, who had sacrificed for his teammates all season long, this otherwise meaningless game against the Pistons was about him. Skywalker came out firing, and he hit nearly everything he put up.

In the first quarter of the game, Skywalker scored a league-record 32 points. He went 13 of 14 from

Thompson pushes the ball up the court and comes within a hair's breadth of the scoring title.

David Thompson (back row, third from the right) poses with the Western Conference All-Stars in 1979.

the field, missing only one shot (a dunk attempt that was blocked) and went six of six from the line. His torrid pace continued in the second quarter, and by halftime he'd scored 53. Determined to shut him down, the Pistons double- and triple-teamed him the rest of the game, limiting Thompson's opportunities. He finished the game 28 of 38 from the field. He had scored 73 points and upped his season scoring average to 27.2 points per game. Unfortunately

for Skywalker, George Gervin scored 63 points that same day, and held on to win the scoring title by seven-hundredths of a point.

Despite Thompson's play, the Nuggets were not able to build on the 1978 season. After a first-round playoff loss in 1979, Larry Brown left

Nomadic Teacher

While he is universally regarded as a great coach, Larry Brown also has a reputation for leaving teams behind. He has coached 14 different teams (collegiate and professional) during his career.

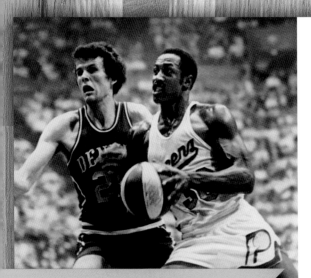

By 1979, George McGinnis' physical style of play had taken its toll.

Denver to coach the UCLA Bruins, and the Nuggets faded back into the pack. Without Coach Brown, they were a team without an identity. Despite the presence of Thompson and Issel, they couldn't manage to outscore opponents. A change was needed. That change began when

Eureka!

McGinnis retired just two years after returning to the Pacers while Alex English starred in Denver for over a decade.

the Nuggets were on the good side of one of the most lopsided trades in NBA history.

George McGinnis is one of the greatest basketball players to ever come out of the state of Indiana. However, by the time he joined the Nuggets for the 1978-79 season, age was catching up with him. While he was only 29 years old, his physical style of play had taken its toll; George was no longer the player he had been. Not recognizing his decline and looking for a spark, the Indiana Pacers decided that bringing the hometown star back to Indiana would energize the team. The Denver Nuggets were only too happy to oblige.

In return for George McGinnis, the Nuggets received 24-year-old forward, and future Hall of Famer, Alex English. In the 1980s, English's talents were on display for all the basketball world to see.

The 1980s are an era remembered for Magic's Lakers, Bird's Celtics, and Dr. J's 76ers. While true fans of the game remember the great player that English was, few realize that during that decade, English scored more points than any other player in the NBA. A soft-spoken yet eloquent man, Alex was often overlooked by a press that desired a big personality. But while Alex may have been a man of few words, his play spoke volumes. In 24 games with Denver in 1980, English averaged 21.3 points per game. It was an impressive debut; it was also the last season that Alex would be held to anything less than 23 points per game for nine years.

Halfway through the 1981 season, the Denver Nuggets decided the team needed a new coach. If Alex English had been the answer to management's prayers, Doug Moe and his up-tempo offense provided a similar boost to the players.

Alex English made frequent trips to the free throw line where he was a career 83% shooter.

Chapter 3
MOE O

Doug Moe played for three ABA All-Star teams in an injury-shortened five-year career.

Doug Moe was raised in Brooklyn, New York. He grew up living and breathing basketball, playing in parks, schools, churches, and everywhere else that he could find an organized game. He was a star player for Coach Dean Smith at the University of North Carolina, and later had a five-year, injury-shortened career in the ABA. Never considered a student of the game, Moe hadn't expected to coach. But one of Moe's best friends, Coach Larry Brown, knew Moe had a way with players and wanted him on his sideline. Moe spent two years as Brown's assistant in Denver before heading to San Antonio and developing a style inspired by his teachers. But it was the differences between his system and his mentors' that got all the attention.

Doug Moe's revolutionary offense was called "the passing game," and it was a style of play that had almost no rules and no plays. It was

Dan Issel gets the shot off over Kevin McHale.

built around crisp ball movement, lots of screens, and constant cuts to the basket. The only rule to running the offense was that players were not allowed to hold the ball for more than two seconds. Moe believed that the sooner his team took a shot, the less chance the defense had to stop it. When he returned to Denver as the head coach, the success of the Nuggets' offense reinforced this belief.

In the modern basketball world, every frame of game film is analyzed. Statistics measure everything from a player's efficiency rating to their rebound rate to their "True Shooting Percentage." In this world, it's hard to imagine a place where a Doug Moe might fit in. However, it wasn't long ago that Doug Moe was completely ignoring game film, inviting players to bring their families and dogs to practice, taking off early to play a round of golf, and winning a Coach of the Year award along the way. Moe once said, "My whole life I've managed to establish myself as a complete fool. Therefore, any success I've had has looked like an upset." While at the time his successes may have looked like upsets, in retrospect

this "complete fool" looks like a basketball genius.

By 1983, David Thompson had been traded to the Seattle SuperSonics. The man once called "Skywalker" had crashed down to earth as a result of personal and physical issues. Thompson was

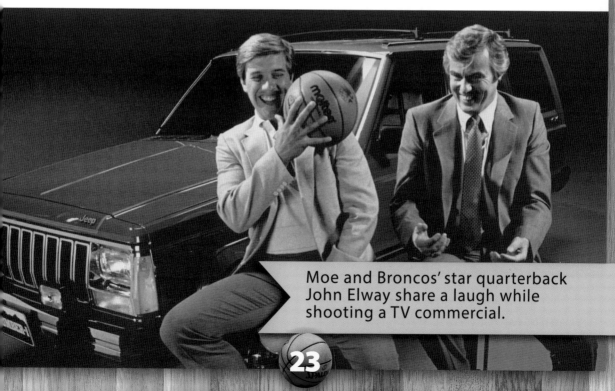

Moe and Broncos' star quarterback John Elway share a laugh while shooting a TV commercial.

unable to recover in time to save his basketball career, but he did overcome his addiction and devote his life to working with young basketball players. In November of 1992, the Denver Nuggets retired Thompson's number 33 uniform in a tearful ceremony at McNichols Sports Arena.

Even without Thompson, the duo of Alex English and Kiki VanDeWeghe led the 1982-83 Nuggets to their first playoff series win since 1978. The team had the league's most potent offense that season, scoring 123.2 points per game. Some complained that they played no defense. But while it was true that their defense had surrendered the most points per game in the league (122.6), Coach Moe was quick to point out that this didn't mean that they were the worst defense. "What people

Doug Moe encourages his young star Kiki VanDeWeghe.

don't realize is that total scores have nothing to do with defense or offense, just the pace of the game. It's the dumbest statistic ever, totally wacko, and yet everyone uses the total scores as an indication of the kind of defense you play. I may not be the smartest guy in the world, but as long as people go by that stat, I know there's someone out there dumber than I am."

Clearly, Coach Moe had his own way of measuring his team's effectiveness. And the more games he won, the more people across the league took notice. In the 1984-85 season, the Nuggets won a division title with a 52-30 record (the team's best since joining the NBA in

Unconventional Offense

Nugget assistant coach Allan Bristow said, "Every offensive set in the passing game is different every time down the court…the only constant is that you take what the defense gives you."

1976). By the time Coach Moe guided Denver all the way to the Western Conference Finals, he could no longer be dismissed as a joke or a

Alex English dunks on Otis Birdsong of the New Jersey Nets.

clown. In fact, other coaches across the league began trying to institute a Moe-style offense on their teams. Of course, the results were disastrous. It seemed that the most important element to a Doug Moe offense was the presence of Doug Moe.

The 1987-88 season may have been Moe's finest in Denver. An intense competitor, Moe was a mild-mannered guy away from the court who enjoyed the company of animals, children, playing golf, and watching movies. By the 1987-88 season, Moe had become a calm presence on the sideline. That season, the Nuggets won 54 games, a Midwest Division title, and Moe was named Coach of the Year. Alex English led the team with 25 points per game while five other players averaged double figures. Sadly, after grabbing a 2-1 series lead against the Dallas Mavericks in the second round, the Nuggets lost three straight and were eliminated from contention.

Doug Moe takes a swing in a game of stickball.

Alex English's 25,613 career points place him #13 on the NBA's all-time scoring-leaders list.

The Alex English/Doug Moe era came to an end in 1990. For both men, the end of their remarkable basketball careers was in sight. For Denver, it was time to rebuild. It would take a couple of years for them to assemble the new stars that would lead the Nuggets back to prominence. The first had a strangely familiar face; the second suffered from a condition that sometimes caused his head to jerk back and to the side as he released his otherwise flawless jump shot; the third brought something the Nuggets hadn't seen in quite a few years—dominant defense.

Poetry—On and Off the Court
Alex English is an accomplished poet who has had three books of his poetry published.

Chapter 4

START ALL OVER AGAIN

The familiar face in Denver in the early to mid-1990s was none other than former Nuggets All Star Dan Issel. As the Nuggets head coach, Issel guided a team led by a pair of top draft picks—Mahmoud Abdul-Rauf and Dikembe Mutombo—back to the playoffs.

A slight, 6' guard from Mississippi, Abdul-Rauf was a terrific shooter with a career free throw percentage of over 90%. He managed to shoot with incredible accuracy despite suffering from a disorder called Tourette's syndrome that causes physical and vocal tics. Abdul-Rauf first began experiencing symptoms of Tourette's as a child, but he did not sit around feeling sorry for himself. Instead he dedicated himself to basketball, working on his shot every day, rain, snow or shine. The undersized Abdul-Rauf was joined by a 7'2" scholar from the Democratic Republic of the Congo, Dikembe Mutombo. Today Mutombo is known for his generosity, for giving millions of dollars to build a hospital near his hometown, the Congolese capital of Kinshasa. But back in the 1990s, it was Mutombo's stinginess

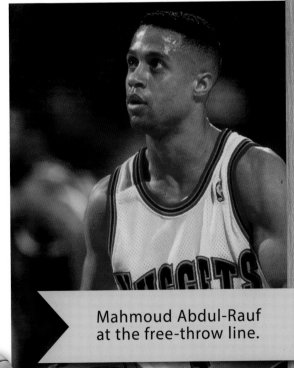

Mahmoud Abdul-Rauf at the free-throw line.

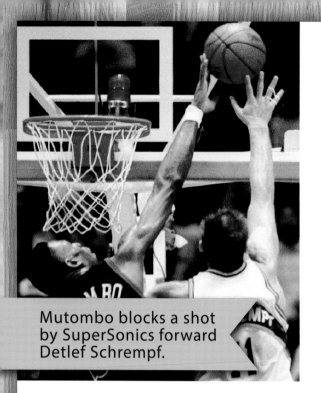

Mutombo blocks a shot by SuperSonics forward Detlef Schrempf.

as one of the NBA's top shot blockers that made him a household name.

The 1993-94 season began with Issel entering his second season as the team's coach. Under his guidance, the Nuggets had made positive strides. In 1992-93, Abdul-Rauf won the Most Improved Player

Flawless Stroke

Abdul-Rauf led the NBA in free throw percentage in 1994, shooting 95.6% from the line.

award, leading the Nuggets with 19 points per game and shooting nearly 94% from the free throw line. His impressive play continued in 1993-94, as did the play of his teammates. Dikembe Mutombo had become one of the game's premiere defenders, averaging 4.1 blocks per game; and LaPhonso Ellis, another top draft pick out of Notre Dame, helped Abdul-Rauf carry the scoring load with 15.4 points per game on 50% shooting from the field. Despite being the youngest team in the league, the Nuggets finished the season with a 42-40 record, good enough to sneak into the playoffs. Unfortunately they were pitted against Gary Payton, Shawn Kemp, and the 63-win Seattle SuperSonics.

The 1994 playoffs started poorly

for Denver. After a Game 2 blowout in Seattle, Sonics fans serenaded their team with chants of "Sweep! Sweep! Sweep!" When asked if he had heard the crowd, Shawn Kemp said: "Oh yeah. If we can go to Denver and sweep and get some rest, I think it'd be good for us." Unfortunately for Kemp and his teammates, Mutombo and the Nuggets heard the chant too. The Nuggets returned home focused and full of fury.

Games 3 and 4 introduced some unlikely heroes. One of the few veterans on the Nuggets, Reggie Williams, exploded for 31 points in Game 3. Denver still needed two more wins to take the series, but fans could sense a shift in momentum. The Nuggets had figured out the tough Sonics defense and Dikembe

Mutombo was terrorizing the Seattle offense, swatting shots back in shooters' faces like a cruel teenager playing a bunch of eight-year-olds.

In Game 4 it was LaPhonso Ellis leading the suddenly confident and revitalized offense to victory with 27 points and 17 rebounds. Mutombo added 16 boards of his own to go along with eight blocks and the SuperSonics were sent back to Seattle, reeling.

Rattled and nervous, the SuperSonics took the floor for Game 5, acutely aware of the kind of history they were trying to avoid. Never before had a #8 seed defeated a #1 seed in the history of the NBA

Denied!
In the 1994 playoffs, Mutombo led all players in blocks per game, averaging 5.75 in 12 games.

Robert Pack gets by Gary Payton during Game 5.

playoffs. This wasn't the kind of "first" the Sonics wanted to be known for.

With Abdul-Rauf struggling to shake free of the larger and stronger Gary "The Glove" Payton, it was back-up point guard Robert Pack who stepped forward in Game 5.

Pesky Eights

Since the Nuggets, two other #8 seeds have beaten a #1 seed: the 2012 Philadelphia 76ers and the 1999 New York Knicks.

Mutombo had eight more blocks, bringing his total to 31 for the series—the most ever in a five-game playoff. But when Seattle made a put-back with half a second to go in regulation to tie the game, it looked like the Nuggets might come up just short. Few outside of Denver had believed the youngest team in the NBA could win a playoff series on the road. Now they would have to do it in overtime.

In the closing seconds of Game 5, with Denver up by four points, the SuperSonics missed a shot and Dikembe Mutombo snatched the rebound. He held the ball high over his head, time expired, and Mutombo fell to the ground, clutching the ball like he'd found gold, and wept tears of joy. Denver had shocked the basketball world. And they still had some surprises in store.

The Denver Nuggets lost the 1994 Western Conference Semifinals to Karl Malone, John Stockton, and the heavily favored Utah Jazz. But they didn't go down without filling Jazz fans with dread. After losing the first three games of the series, the Nuggets caught fire, beating the Jazz in three straight to even the series. Had the Nuggets won Game 7 and come back from the 0-3 hole, they would have been the first team to do so in the history of the NBA. Alas, it was not meant to be. Utah held on to win Game 7 and the 1994 Denver Nuggets had to be satisfied with one historical achievement.

Historic Comebacks

No NBA team has ever come back from a 3-0 deficit to win a best-of-seven playoff series, but eight have rallied back from 3-1 and 15 from 2-0.

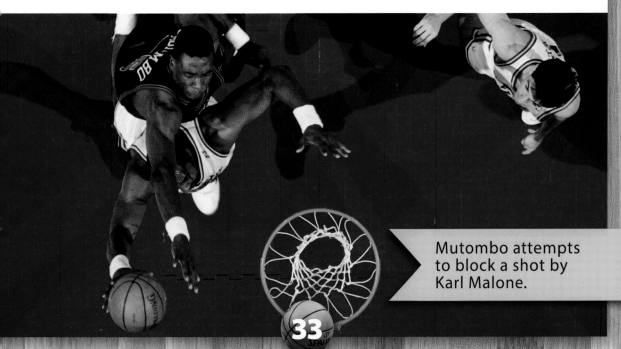

Mutombo attempts to block a shot by Karl Malone.

While history-making is entertaining, Nuggets fans had grown to expect more than one good run. And while the Nuggets had yet to win a championship, they'd rarely suffered through long droughts where they didn't make the playoffs. But following the 1994 playoffs, the Nuggets experienced a series of disappointing seasons. Players such as Dale Ellis, Jalen Rose, and Antonio McDyess were brought to Denver to help right the ship, but basketball is a mysterious game. Talent is not always enough. Winning requires having players whose style and leadership skills complement one another. Before long, Mutombo, Abdul-Rauf, and Ellis would all be gone, along with the players brought in to help them achieve greatness.

Following the 1994-95 season, the Nuggets would fail to qualify for the playoffs for eight straight years. During that period, the success of the Denver Broncos—winners of back-to-back Super Bowls—would outshine the Nuggets completely. John Elway and Terrell Davis were Denver's champions. The Nuggets were an afterthought. By April 2003, the

A devastating knee injury suffered in 2001 caused Antonio McDyess to miss nearly two full seasons.

Nuggets had reached a low point, finishing the regular season in last place with a paltry 17 wins. But their poor finish was enough to earn them the third pick in the draft. And the 2003 NBA Draft was loaded with talent.

The Nuggets' savior arrived express from Syracuse University where, as a freshman, he had just led the Orangemen to their first national championship. At 6'8" and 230 pounds he was big, strong, swift, and he could score from anywhere on the floor. His teammates called him Melo.

Carmelo Anthony was born in the Red Hook housing projects of Brooklyn, New York. When he was two years old, he lost his father to cancer,

and when he was eight, he and his mother moved to West Baltimore. In the rough neighborhoods in which he grew up, basketball was more than just a game; it was a method of survival. By immersing himself in the game he loved, Melo was able

Carmelo Anthony was named the 2003 NCAA Tournament's Most Outstanding Player.

to avoid trouble and stay focused on his goals.

In a draft that included LeBron James, Dwyane Wade, and Chris Bosh, Denver Nuggets general manager and former star, Kiki VanDeWeghe, selected Carmelo Anthony with the third pick. In the 2003-04 season, the 19-year-old Carmelo averaged 21 points, six rebounds, and three assists per game. It was clear that what the Nuggets needed was a supporting cast for their new superstar.

The 2003-04 Denver Nuggets won 43 games against 39 losses. They became the first team ever to make the playoffs following a season in which they had less than 20 wins. While they were knocked out of the playoffs in the first round by Kevin Garnett's Minnesota Timberwolves, it was still a huge step forward for the franchise. The next step forward came in December of 2004, when the team hired George Karl as their new head coach.

Under Karl's tutelage, the Nuggets steadily improved over the next few seasons. But in the powerful Western Conference, they never managed to escape the first round of the playoffs. In 2006, feeling that Melo needed help with the scoring load, the team acquired former MVP Allen Iverson from Philadelphia. In one sense, the move worked. For two seasons, Melo and Iverson were

Historic Class

The 2003 NBA Draft is widely considered to be the best since the 1984 Draft that included Jordan, Olajuwon, Barkley, and Stockton.

the highest scoring duo in the NBA. The Nuggets finished the 2007-08 season with 50 wins for the first time since 1987. But in a loaded Western Conference, 50 wins were just barely enough to make the playoffs. The 2007-08 50-win Nuggets earned a #8 seed in the playoffs and were eliminated in the first round for the fifth straight season. Something had to change.

The change that took the Nuggets to the next level was the trade of Allen Iverson to Detroit for hometown hero Chauncey Billups. Born in Denver, Chauncey had been Mr. Colorado Basketball three times at George Washington High School. Given numerous options, Billups had decided to stay nearby for college, and he became a star

Mr. Big Shot returns to Denver.

guard at the University of Colorado. While his first few years in the NBA were bumpy, Chauncey found himself in Minnesota with the help of players like Terrell Brandon and Kevin Garnett. By the time Chauncey returned to Denver, he had led the Detroit Pistons to an NBA title, been voted the Finals MVP, and earned a fitting nickname: "Mr. Big Shot."

Chapter 5

A Memorable Run and a Law-Abiding Future

In 2009, the Denver Nuggets climbed their way to the #2 seed in the Western Conference. Once again the Western Conference was stacked with outstanding teams. The difference between the #2 and the #8 seed was a mere six games. As the #2 seed, one might expect that the Nuggets would be a huge favorite against their first-round opponent, but this was not the case. The #7 seed New Orleans Hornets had two All-Stars in Chris Paul and David West. Nuggets fans, so eager to see their team advance beyond the first round, had to be nervous about the match up. The season before, the Hornets had won 56 games and advanced to the Western Conference Semifinals. They were talented and experienced. But thanks to the presence of Chauncey Billups, the Nuggets had something the Hornets could not boast–a Finals MVP.

To the delight of Nuggets fans, Denver won their first two games at home and grabbed a 2-0 series lead. But when the teams traveled to New

Nuggets' power forward Kenyon Martin celebrates a dunk and Nuggets fans go wild.

Mr. Big Shot gets by Dirk Nowitzki for the layup.

team before Game 4 worked. The Nuggets crushed the Hornets in New Orleans 121-63, tying the record for the biggest blowout in the history of the NBA playoffs. They finished off the demoralized Hornets in Game 5 and continued their hot play in the second round against Dirk Nowitzki's Dallas Mavericks. Melo averaged 30 points per game against Dallas and the Nuggets cruised past the Mavs in five games, advancing to the Conference Finals for the first time since 1985.

Orleans, the Hornets won Game 3. Having coached the SuperSonics during their epic collapse against the Nuggets in 1994, George Karl had no interest in going down that road again. Whatever he said to his

The Denver Nuggets were not crowned champions of the Western Conference in 2009, but they made an impression on the rest of the league. After suffering a series of frustrating first-round playoff losses, they finally emerged as one of the league's premiere teams. They had always competed with the big boys in the regular season, and now they were doing it in the "second season." In Game 2 of the Western Conference Finals in Los Angeles, Melo and Chauncey went for 34 and 27 respectively, and the Nuggets stole home court from the Lakers—despite 32 points from Kobe Bryant. It looked like they might have a shot to go all the way to the NBA Finals. But while they were able stay even with L.A. through four games, the Lakers won Games 5 and 6 to take the series. The Nuggets thrilling run was over, but they were far from discouraged. As far as they were concerned, they'd proven themselves worthy. Their

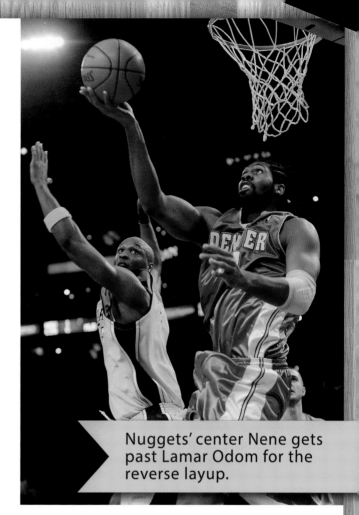

Nuggets' center Nene gets past Lamar Odom for the reverse layup.

next goal was a championship.

Sadly for Denver, the next season-and-a-half only provided more

30, 30, 30, 30, 30 Club
During the Western Conference Finals, Carmelo became the first Nugget ever to score 30 or more points in five straight playoff games.

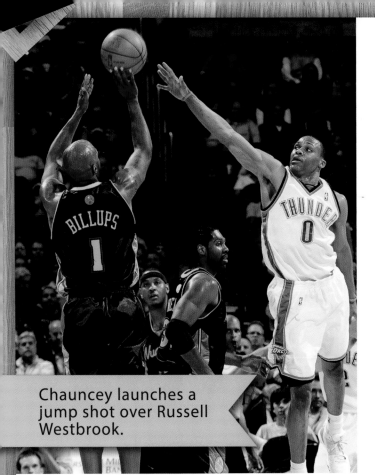

Chauncey launches a jump shot over Russell Westbrook.

Even with the addition of an exciting young point guard in Ty Lawson to back up Chauncey, even with Carmelo raising his scoring average to 28 points per game, the Nuggets couldn't get past Deron Williams and the Utah Jazz.

In the 2010-11 season, the Carmelo Anthony era ended. After being told by Carmelo that he would not resign with the team when his contract was up, the Nuggets traded Melo and Chauncey Billups to New York for a handful of young standouts. It was a massive overhaul, and Denver fans wondered how long it would take for their team to compete again at a high level. They didn't have to

disappointment. Having seemingly figured out how to advance past the first round in 2009, the 2010 Nuggets reverted to their old ways.

Good Company

Melo left the Nuggets as the third-highest scorer in team history behind Dan Issel and the Nuggets' all-time scoring leader Alex English.

Gallinari and Chandler after a midseason wardrobe change.

wait long for their answer. The next season, players such as Gallinari, Chandler, Andre Miller, and Arron Afflalo helped lead the Nuggets right back to the top of the Western Conference. They followed a young, lightning-quick floor general whose star was on the rise.

The fact that the 2012-13 Denver Nuggets had nine players averaging between eight and 16 points per game said a lot about their unselfishness. That unselfishness started with their leader, 5'11" point guard Ty Lawson. In a league of superhuman athletes, few players are as explosive off the dribble as Ty. As his jump shot has improved, he's become one of the hardest players in the NBA to stop. And he works just as hard on defense as he does on offense. In 2009, Ty set the record for steals in the NCAA national title game with eight, leading the North Carolina Tar Heels to the National Championship. In the NBA, his habit of thievery has continued.

In the 2012-13 season, Lawson led a cast of characters that included Kenneth Faried, Wilson Chandler, Danilo Gallinari, JaVale McGee and Andre Iguodala to an NBA franchise-record 57 wins. While the Nuggets lost a heartbreaking first-round series to the Golden State Warriors, they have reason to be hopeful entering the 2013-14 season.

2013 saw the departure of George Karl and Andre Iguodala from Denver. They will not be easily replaced. But in the 2013-14 season, Denver fans can anticipate the arrival of a coach who players have been hyping since Phil Jackson stepped down as the head coach of the Los Angeles Lakers.

After a lengthy career as a point guard for numerous

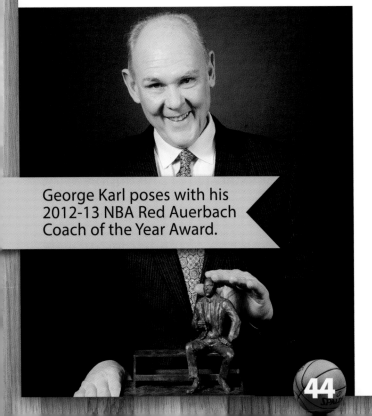

George Karl poses with his 2012-13 NBA Red Auerbach Coach of the Year Award.

teams, Brian Shaw spent eight years as an assistant to Phil Jackson in Los Angeles. There he helped coach the Lakers to three consecutive NBA titles. Lakers great Shaquille O'Neal has said that Shaw was the teammate he had the most respect for throughout his career. Scores of other players have concurred. As Shaw prepares for his first season as a head coach, he does so with the full confidence of Nuggets players, ownership, and new general manager Tim Connelly. When asked what the focus for the 2013-14 season will be, Shaw said, "Playoff basketball is the main focus, improved half-court offense and defense are key, and playing the

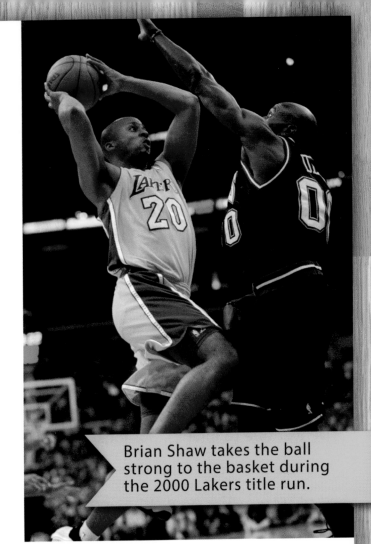

Brian Shaw takes the ball strong to the basket during the 2000 Lakers title run.

youngsters is paramount to success." His words were music to the ears of Nuggets fans everywhere.

Looking at the 2013-14 Denver Nuggets, it's hard to choose a player to profile. A terrific scorer with the

Brian Shaw (middle) with Nuggets' General Manager and Executive Vice President of Basketball Operations Tim Connelly (left) and President Josh Kroenke (right).

Knicks, Wilson Chandler has had limited opportunities to excel in Denver due to injuries. But look for the athletic 6'8" Chandler—who shot over 41% from three-point range in 2012-13—to have his best years as a pro ahead of him.

Danilo Gallinari missed the 2013 playoffs with an ACL injury. Had the 6'10" forward, with the ability to drain threes or put the ball on the floor and get to the rim, not been injured, who knows where the Nuggets might have gone in 2013.

Standing seven feet tall with a 7'6" wingspan and a 33" vertical leap, it's safe to say that the NBA has never seen anyone like JaVale McGee. In past seasons, the Nuggets have seen flashes of brilliance from their young center. In 2013-14, the Nuggets will look for consistency from McGee, something he has yet to display in a Denver uniform.

New additions J.J. Hickson, Randy Foye, and three-time Slam Dunk champion, Nate Robinson, will certainly provide an offensive boost. Hickson is known for his ability to crash the offensive boards and get points around the rim, while Foye and Robinson can light it up from outside.

Then there is Kenneth Faried. Whatever his role, Faried will lead

by example. One needs only to look at the way he stepped forward to support Jason Collins, the NBA's first openly gay player, to know what kind of a teammate he is. Raised by his mother to work his tail off and rebound the basketball, Faried's big heart has been on display from

Nate Robinson soars to Slam Dunk championship #2.

the moment he put on a Nuggets uniform. His physical style of play has earned him the nickname "Manimal," and in his third year in the league, look for the Manimal to continue to

Kenneth Faried skies for the rebound amongst a throng of Thunder players.

battle on every play and be on the receiving end of alley-oops from Lawson.

The Denver Nuggets have been a very good team for a long time. In the past six years, they've won 50 or more games five times, and they've qualified for the playoffs 10 years in a row. And yet, when many think of the Denver Nuggets, it's as a good team, nothing more. It's time for that to change. Fifty wins are no longer good enough. With a promising young coach, a brilliant general manager, and a cast of unselfish players who possess a combination of strength and speed that few teams in the NBA can match, the Nuggets are aiming Mile High.